The Beginnings of Monkey

Adapted by Xu Li
from the novel *Journey to the West*
Illustrated by Lu Xinsen

FOREIGN LANGUAGES PRESS   BEIJING

First Edition 1985

Hard Cover: ISBN 0-8351-1317-5
Paperback: ISBN 0-8351-1316-7

Published by the Foreign Languages Press
24 Baiwanzhuang Road, Beijing, China

Distributed by China International Book Trading Corporation
(Guoji Shudian), P.O. Box 399, Beijing, China

Printed in the People's Republic of China

Long, long ago there was a country named Aolai in the Eastern Continent. This country was by an ocean, and in the middle of the ocean was an island called the Mountain of Flowers and Fruit, a mountain with crystal spring water, pines, cypresses, exotic flowers and fruit trees. On the top of this mountain there was a magic stone.

Ever since creation, this stone had been shone on by the sun and the moon and moistened by rain and dew. One day there was suddenly a great noise as the stone split and a stone egg jumped out. When the wind blew on it this egg turned into a stone monkey.

Everything was new to the baby monkey. He was curious about everything and learned to crawl and walk. Soon he was able to run and jump, eat wild fruit and drink from streams.

The stone monkey made friends with other monkeys. One day they saw a waterfall just like a door curtain in front of a cliff. One monkey said, "If anyone is clever enough to go through the fall, find where the water comes from and get out again in one piece, let's make him our king."

When this challenge had been shouted three times, the stone monkey leaped out from the crowd and answered at the top of his voice, "I'll go, I'll go!" Then he shut his eyes, crouched, and sprang straight into the waterfall.

When he opened his eyes and looked round, he saw an iron bridge in front of him. On one side of the bridge there was a stone cave. Then he noticed a stone tablet on which was carved: HAPPY LAND OF THE MOUNTAIN OF FLOWERS AND FRUIT, CAVE HEAVEN OF THE WATER CURTAIN.

Inside the cave were stone beds, a stone stove, a stone table and stone benches and chairs. On the stone table were stone plates and stone bowls. The stone monkey was very happy. "This is really a wonderful place," he said. "There's room for thousands of us here. Let's all move in, then we won't have to put up with any more nonsense from heaven."

The stone monkey hurried out and jumped back through the water curtain. He told the other monkeys about what he had seen in the cave. The others were all delighted and asked the stone monkey to let them in to have a look. Then the stone monkey leaped in again, shouting, "Follow me!" The other monkeys all jumped through.

The monkeys all grabbed plates, snatched bowls, bagged beds and fought over chairs. They found some wine and peaches for a feast, then lined up to pay homage, calling the stone monkey "Your Majesty the King". Then the stone monkey took the throne and called himself the Handsome Monkey King.

The Handsome Monkey King took control of his monkeys, apes, gibbons and
others, and chose some as his ministers and officials. Every morning they roamed
the Mountain of Flowers and Fruit and spent each night in the Water Curtain
Cave. They ate fruits when they were hungry and drank from springs when
thirsty. They had their own king, and they thoroughly enjoyed themselves.

This happy life lasted for hundreds of years. But one day the Handsome Monkey King suddenly felt miserable and started crying. The monkeys were worried and they asked, "What's the matter, Your Majesty?" "Although we're happy now," the Monkey King replied, "one day we'll be old and die." When the monkeys heard this they all covered their faces and wept.

A gibbon came forward and said, "Don't upset yourself, Your Majesty. We can ask the immortals to teach us how to live forever." "Where do they live?" Monkey asked. The ape thought for a moment and replied, "People say they live in ancient caves on magic mountains."

The Monkey King was very pleased. Straight away he ordered the other monkeys to cut bamboo and trees to make a raft and gather fruit for him to eat on his voyage. He was to sail the oceans and go to the edge of the sky to find the immortals and discover the secret of eternal life.

The next day the monkeys set out to pick magic peaches, rare fruits and flowers. Everything was put on the stone benches and the stone table, with other magic food and wine. The monkeys led the Handsome Monkey King to the seat of honour and sat down below him. Each of them took turns to bring him wine and fruit, and they drank for a whole day.

The next morning the Handsome Monkey King went aboard the raft, pushed off hard, and floated off on the ocean waves. The other monkeys stood on the seashore, sad to see him go.

The Handsome Monkey King on his raft was eager to find a teacher. Some days later the wind blew him to the shore of the Southern Continent.

One day the Handsome Monkey King reached the shores of the Southern Sea. He saw some people moving around. He went up to them and found they were busy fishing and making nets. When they saw him they were so scared that they dropped their baskets and nets and fled.

The Monkey King grabbed one of them who was a slow runner, took his clothes, and dressed himself in them so that he looked like a human. He swaggered towards the market place.

The Handsome Monkey King was very clever. When he was with people he peered around and took an interest in everything. He soon learned to talk, walk and behave just like a human. He went to many towns and villages, and before he realized it eight or nine years had passed.

Although he asked about immortal gods and Buddhas, the Monkey King was unable to meet one. He was very worried about this, and when one day he reached the Great Western Ocean he thought that there must be immortals on the other side of it. He made himself another raft and floated across the Western Ocean until he came to the Western Continent.

In the distance he saw mountains and cliffs. Then he heard singing and chopping coming from the depths of the forest. He went ashore and met a woodcutter. "Old Immortal, your disciple greets you," he said. The woodcutter replied, "No, no. I don't even have enough to eat or drink. You can't call me an immortal."

The Monkey King asked the woodcutter to show him where the immortals lived. The woodcutter said, "Not far from here is the Cave of the Setting Moon and Three Stars, where an immortal called the Patriarch Subhuti lives. If you follow that path south for two or three miles you'll reach his home." The Monkey King left the woodcutter and went deep into the mountains.

The Monkey King crossed a hill and saw a cave. The doors were closed. He turned round and noticed that there was a stone tablet carved in enormous letters: SPIRIT TOWER HEART MOUNTAIN, CAVE OF THE SETTING MOON AND THREE STARS. The Monkey King was delighted but did not dare to knock on the door. He climbed to the end of a pine branch and ate some pine nuts.

After a while the doors of the cave opened with a creak, and an immortal boy came out. The Monkey King scrambled down from the tree. The boy asked, "Have you come to ask about the Way and study under the immortals?" "Yes," the Monkey King replied. "Our master has just mounted the dais to teach the Way," said the boy. "He told me to take you in. Will you come with me?"

The Monkey King tidied himself up and followed the boy in. In the depths of the cave there were wonderful flowers, majestic pavilions, towers of red jade, pearl palaces, cowrie gateways, silent rooms and secluded cells. After passing all these he reached a jasper dais.

The Patriarch Subhuti was sitting on the dais and several dozen immortal boys were standing on either side. The Monkey King bowed and said, "Master, I have crossed the oceans and travelled for over ten years to reach here. Would you in your mercy take me as your disciple?"

The Patriarch opened his eyes slowly and asked with a smile, "Where are you from? What's your name?" "I come from the Water Curtain Cave on the Mountain of Flowers and Fruit in the land of Aolai in the Eastern Continent," answered Monkey. "I have neither name nor parents. I was born from a stone. Could you give me a name?"

The Patriarch said, "Walk around for a moment and let me have a look at you."
The Monkey King leaped to his feet and shambled round a couple of times. The
Patriarch smiled and said, "You have rather an ugly body, and you look like one
of the monkeys that eat pine nuts, so I ought to give you a name that fits your
appearance. I'll call you Sun Wukong. Will that do?" "Marvellous, marvellous,"
said the Monkey King with a smile. He thanked the Patriarch many times.

The Monkey King bowed to all the older disciples. From then on he learned the correct ways to speak and act from them, discussed the scriptures and the Way, practised his handwriting and burned incense. Every day he got up early and went to bed late. He studied very hard.

Apart from his spiritual training the Monkey King also swept the floor, dug the vegetable patch, grew flowers, tended the trees, fetched kindling, lit the fire, carried water and chopped wood. He worked very hard.

Every three days the Monkey King and the other disciples practised with swords, spears, knives and cudgels. He was the best of them all. Several years slipped by in the cave in this way without him noticing.

One day the Patriarch took his seat on the dais and began to explain the Great Way. As Monkey sat at the side listening he was so delighted that he tugged at his ear, scratched his cheek and smiled. When the Patriarch noticed this he said to Monkey, "Why don't you listen to me quietly?" "I have been listening to what you're saying with all my attention," Monkey replied, "but your marvellous words made me so happy that I started to move about without realizing what I was doing. Please forgive me."

The Patriarch asked, "How long have you been in my cave?" Monkey replied, "I have no idea. All I know is that when I'm sent out to collect firewood I go to the other side of the mountain and have had seven good feeds of peaches there." Then the Patriarch said, "If you have eaten there seven times you must have been here seven years. What sort of Way do you want to learn from me?" "That depends what you teach me, Master. Your disciple will learn anything as long as there's a whiff of Way to it."

The Patriarch said, "What about teaching you the Way of magic arts? The magic arts include summoning immortals, fortune telling and divination. You can use them to make good things happen and prevent bad ones." "That can't help me to become immortal, so I won't learn it," Sun Wukong replied. "Shall I teach you the Way of Silence?" the Patriarch then asked. "That's not the way to become an immortal either, so I won't learn that," Monkey answered.

When the Patriarch heard this he lost his temper and climbed down from his dais. Pointing at Sun Wukong with his cane he said, "You won't study this and you won't study that, so what do you want, you monkey?" He went over to Monkey and hit him three times on the head, then went inside with his hands behind his back. He shut the main door, leaving them all.

The class was shocked, and they were all cross with Sun Wukong. "You cheeky ape, you've no idea how to behave. The master was teaching you the Way, so why did you have to argue with him instead of learning from him?" But Sun Wukong was not bothered in the least, and his face was covered with smiles.

Back in his room the Monkey King took his seat and waited impatiently for night to come. When it was about the third watch, or midnight, and all the others were sound asleep, Monkey slipped out and tiptoed to the back door, which he found ajar. He was delighted.

Monkey walked over to the Patriarch's bedroom, where he saw the Patriarch lying fast asleep. Not daring to disturb him, Sun Wukong knelt in front of the bed.

Before long the Patriarch woke up and shouted, "What are you here for, Wukong?" Monkey replied, "Master, when you hit me three times that meant to come at the third watch, and when you went inside with your hands behind your back and shut the main door that told me to go in through the back door for you to teach me the Way in secret. So I've come and been kneeling here for a long time."

The Patriarch was very pleased to hear this and realized that this monkey was indeed exceptional. "Since you understood my hidden message," he said, "come over here and listen carefully while I teach you the miraculous Way of Immortality."

Afterwards, every night at the third watch, Monkey came into the cave to learn the Way from the Patriarch and went back to his bed before dawn without the others knowing. After three years had passed in this way Monkey had learned from his master the seventy-two transformations.

The Patriarch also taught Monkey the art of flying and somersaulting on a cloud. With one somersault Monkey could cover sixty thousand miles.

One day in early summer, when all the disciples were talking about the Great Way and immortals, the other disciples asked, "Sun Wukong, the other day our teacher taught you how to do transformations to avoid the Three Disasters. Can you show us some?"

"Yes," Monkey answered cockily, "first I'll show you a somersault cloud and then the seventy-two transformations." All the others nodded. Monkey said the magic words, jumped head over heels, and was soon out of sight.

An instant later he reappeared with a grin and said, "I went sixty thousand miles." Then he clenched his fist, said another spell, shook himself, and changed into a pine tree.

As the disciples were standing under the tree they couldn't see clearly when it changed into a white crane that flew over and landed on the ground to greet them.

When the disciples saw it they clapped their hands and cheered. They didn't realize that the row they were making had disturbed the Patriarch, who rushed out and asked, "Who's making that row?" All the disciples knelt and said, "We were cheering because Wukong did some transformations just now. We beg you to forgive us for disturbing you, Master."

Seeing Monkey couldn't behave himself, the Patriarch worried that this would
lead to serious trouble, so he sent them all away except for Sun Wukong. "You
can't stay here for long, or your life will be in danger," he said. "Go back to
where you came from."

Monkey kowtowed and said, "Please forgive me, Master. I have not yet done anything to thank you for your kindness to me over the years. I can't bring myself to go." Then the Patriarch said, "What sort of favour would you be doing me by staying? I'll be grateful enough if you keep me out of any trouble you get into."

"Now that you're going," the Patriarch added, "I'm sure that you will cause trouble. I forbid you under any circumstances to call yourself my disciple. If you so much as hint at it I'll know at once, and I'll skin you, chop up your bones, and make sure you never recover." "I'll do what you say," Sun Wukong replied. Then he changed his clothes and said goodbye to his master and the other disciples.

Sun Wukong went down the mountain. He missed the home he'd been away from for twenty years and his children and grandchildren, so he said the spell and went straight by somersault through the clouds to the Mountain of Flowers and Fruit.

Within two hours he could see the Water Curtain Cave on the Mountain of Flowers and Fruit. He looked down and saw that everything was in ruins. There was not a single flower or fruit tree in front of the cave. He could hear cranes and apes crying and howling.

Coming round to the front of the cave Monkey shouted, "Children, I'm back." At this thousands and thousands of monkeys came bounding from caves in the cliffs, from holes in the ground, and down from the trees. They all crowded round the Monkey King, weeping bitterly.

Monkey asked them what had happened. "Two years ago," the monkeys replied, "the Demon King of Confusion came from the Cave in the Belly of the Water in the northern mountains. He's taken our Water Curtain Cave, and we've been fighting for our lives with him. But we can't beat him. He's been stealing our things and carrying off many of our youngsters. If you hadn't come back we'd have all been done for."

Sun Wukong was furious. "Don't worry," he said, "I'm going to catch that demon king." Then he jumped up into the air, and as he somersaulted towards the north he saw a high and steep mountain. There was a cave facing a cliff, and over the cave was carved: THE CAVE IN THE BELLY OF THE WATER.

Several young devils were dancing around in front of the entrance, and they ran away as soon as they saw Monkey. "I'm the king of the Water Curtain Cave in the Mountain of Flowers and Fruit," said Monkey, "and I've come to have it out with that Demon King of Confusion of yours who's been bullying my children and grandchildren."

A junior devil scuttled into the cave and reported, "A disaster, Your Majesty. There's a monkey outside the cave, who says that he's the king of the Water Curtain Cave on the Mountain of Flowers and Fruit. He says that you've been bullying his children and grandchildren, and that he's come to have it out with you."

The demon king, who was drinking, laughed and said, "Those monkey devils are always going on about a king of theirs who went away to become an immortal; I suppose he must be here now. Did you see how he was dressed or what weapons he was carrying?" "He hasn't got any weapons," the junior devil replied. "He's bare-headed and isn't dressed like a monk or an immortal. He's standing outside the doors, yelling."

The demon king ordered his junior devils to fetch his armour and sword and went outside with all his army of devils.

Seeing that Monkey was very small and unarmed, the demon king put his sword down and got ready to box Monkey. "Come on then!" said Monkey, jumping up and hitting the demon in the face.

After several rounds the demon king had been beaten black and blue. He flew into a rage and shouted, "I wasn't paying attention just then. Let's have another round." Sun Wukong didn't say a single word but punched him in the eyes, then kicked his ribs. The demon king fell to the ground.

All the junior devils surrounded Monkey, who jumped over them and got out.
Then all the devils bumped into each other.

The demon king stood up and struck at Monkey's head with his sword. Monkey dodged out of the way. The demon struck again, but Monkey had disappeared. There was laughter behind the demon king.

The demon king was desperate as he turned round to strike again. Seeing how ugly the demon king had turned, Sun Wukong used his magic art of making extra bodies. He pulled out some of his hairs, popped them into his mouth, chewed them up, and blew them out, shouting, "Change!" They turned into several hundred little monkeys, who all charged towards the demon king.

Since Sun Wukong had learned the Way he could change each of the eighty-four thousand hairs on his body into anything he wanted. All the monkeys leaped and jumped about, rushing up and surrounding the demon king, grabbing, seizing, poking him in the backside, pulling at his feet, punching him, scratching at his eyes and throwing him to the ground.

Monkey snatched the demon king's sword from him, told the little monkeys to get out of the way, and cut the demon king into two. Then he led the monkeys into the cave, where they killed all the devils.

Sun Wukong shook himself and put the hairs back on his body. Then he told the monkeys he had rescued from the demon king to set fire to the Cave in the Belly of the Water and burn it out. After that Monkey told the little monkeys to shut their eyes, recited a spell, summoned a somersault cloud and took them back to the Mountain of Flowers and Fruit.

All the little monkeys laid on a feast to celebrate their king's return. Monkey told his children how he travelled across the Eastern and Western Oceans to learn the Great Way and how he had defeated the demon king and saved them. Then he laughed and said, "Children, we have a surname now. My surname is Sun, and my Buddhist name is Wukong. I give all of you a surname — Sun!" All the monkeys clapped and were happy.

The Handsome Monkey King had captured the Demon King of Confusion's sword. He told the little monkeys to cut down bamboo to make spears, and to carve wooden swords. They practised with them every day.

One day Monkey thought that if demons or ghosts came the monkeys would be no match for them with their bamboo spears and wooden swords. They needed really sharp weapons. Four older monkeys made a suggestion, "To the east of our mountain there is a country called Aolai. There must be weapons there, but we have no gold and silver to buy them."

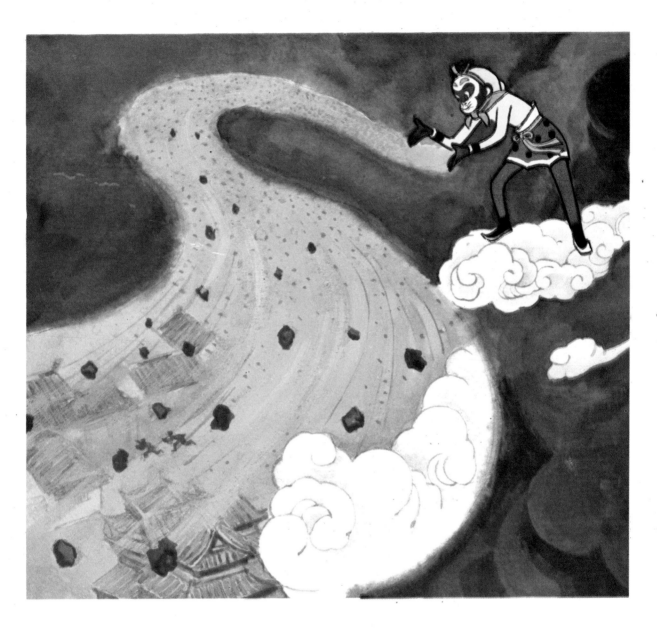

Monkey was delighted. "Wait here while I go and get some weapons," he said. He leaped onto his somersault cloud and soon arrived in the sky over Aolai. He made magic with his fist and said the words of a spell. Suddenly a terrifying gale and sandstorm started. The people of Aolai were so frightened that they shut their doors. Nobody dared to go outside.

Monkey landed his cloud and rushed straight in through the gates of the palace to the military stores, where he found all eighteen sorts of weapons. He plucked a handful of hairs from his body, chewed them up, and spat them out. They turned into hundreds and thousands of little monkeys who carried all the weapons away.

Monkey climbed back up on the clouds and took all the little monkeys home with him. At the sight of the weapons, all the monkeys on the Mountain of Flowers and Fruit were delighted. They snatched swords, grabbed spears, seized battle-axes, and fought for pikes. They shouted, yelled, and played around with them for the rest of the day.

From then on the Water Curtain Cave on the Mountain of Flowers and Fruit became famous. The monster kings all came to pay homage to the Monkey King. They took part in drill or offered presents and grain taxes. Colourful flags flew over the Mountain of Flowers and Fruit, and drums and gongs were beaten. But trouble was ahead for Monkey. He would not be able to stay long in his paradise.

美猴王丛书

孙悟空出世

许　力　改编

陆新森　绘画

＊

外文出版社出版

（中国北京百万庄路24号）

人民教育出版社印刷厂印刷

中国国际图书贸易总公司

（中国国际书店）发行

北京399信箱

1985年（16开）第一版

编号：（英）8050－2557

00500　（精）

00400　（平）

88－E－261